coolcareers.com

Webmaster

Marty Brown

the rosen publishing group's
rosen central
new york

For Alexander Robinson Schultz, master of all he surveys.

Published in 2000 by The Rosen Publishing Group, Inc.
29 East 21st Street, New York, NY 10010

Library of Congress Cataloging-in-Publication Data

Brown, Marty, 1966–
    Webmaster / Marty Brown
       p. 22 cm. — (Coolcareers.com)
    Includes bibliographical references and index.
    Summary: This book discusses the career of a Webmaster, including the skills needed, the opportunities for work, and the challenges for the future.
    ISBN 0-8239-3111-0 (lib. bdg.)
    1. Web sites—Design—Vocational guidance—Juvenile literature. 2. Webmasters—Vocational guidance—Juvenile literature. [1. Web sites. 2. World Wide Web (informational retrieval system). 3. Vocational guidance.]
    005.2'76—dc21

Manufactured in the United States of America

CONTENTS

ABOUT THIS BOOK

Technology is changing all the time. Just a few years ago, hardly anyone who wasn't a hardcore technogeek had heard of the Internet or the World Wide Web. Computers and modems were way slower and less powerful. If you said "dot com," no one would have any idea what you meant. Hard to imagine, isn't it?

It is also hard to imagine how much more change and growth is possible in the world of technology. People who work in the field are busy imagining, planning, and working toward the future, but even they can't be sure how computers and the Internet will look and function by the time you are ready to start your career. This book is intended to give you an idea of what is out there now so that you can think about what interests you and how to find out more about it.

One thing is clear: Computer-related occupations will continue to increase in number and variety. The demand for qualified workers in these extremely cool fields is increasing all the time. So if you want to get a head start on the competition, or if you just like to fool around with computers, read on!

chapter one

WHY BE A WEBMASTER?

If you haven't seen the World Wide Web, you need to stay in more. It's only the hottest destination on the Internet (and if you haven't heard of the Internet, come out from under your rock). Every year, more and more people turn to the Web for information, recreation, and entertainment. As of 1999, the number of active Web sites on the Internet was estimated at about five million, and the number is growing every year.

And that's just on the Internet. There are also countless Web sites on private computer networks called intranets. These Web sites are used by businesses and organizations for internal communications and for collaboration between work groups. Just like the Internet, intranet use has exploded in the past few years, and as if that weren't enough,

The need for Webmasters increases every day.

another category of Web sites, called extranets, is starting to emerge.

As the Web grows at a furious pace with no slowdown in sight, the need for qualified people to design, build, and maintain Web sites grows just as fast. So who builds and maintains all those Web sites?

Webmasters.

Not only is there a big need for Webmasters, but it's a fun and challenging career. A good Webmaster needs a wide range of skills, from computer networking and programming knowledge to writing and communications skills to an eye for graphic design. Depending on where you work, you might specialize in just one of these aspects of Web development, or you might wear all of these hats at once.

Almost as diverse as the skills you need are the places you might work. Businesses, governments, schools, nonprofit organizations—organizations of all types, shapes, and sizes—need Webmasters. If you're the independent type, you might prefer to go it alone and work as a freelance Web developer. The possibilities are enormous and are growing every day.

All types of organizations and companies need Webmasters.

IT'S TOO TECHNICAL FOR ME... ▶▶

Even if you're not a "technical person," you might be very well suited to a career as a Webmaster. Sure, the Web uses a lot of technology, but that's nothing to be intimidated by. The Web is all about communication and about sharing information; it's about informing, educating, and entertaining people.

It has as much in common with traditional media fields—publishing, broadcasting, advertising, and marketing—as it does with computer science. The Web takes a little bit from all of those areas, but it's not exactly like anything else.

SO WHAT EXACTLY IS THE WEB?

There's nothing exact about the Web. It is a lot of different things to a lot of different people. On the Internet alone, there is a dizzying variety of things to choose from. There are on-line storefronts, also called e-commerce sites, which sell products directly to consumers, much like traditional mail-order catalogs. There are publications, such as newspapers and magazines, that deliver all their articles on-line.

Lots of shopping, or e-commerce, takes place on the Web.

There are Web-based brochures that businesses use for marketing and public relations. There are phone directories, library catalogs, audio and video collections, dictionaries, interactive networked games, and a whole lot of other stuff that you've never even thought of. Although they're not visible to the general public, intranets and extranets are just as diverse. One thing all these Web sites have in common is this: They all need Webmasters.

WHAT DOES A WEBMASTER NEEED TO KNOW? ▶▶▶▶▶▶▶▶▶

What you need to know to be a Webmaster depends to a very large extent on the type of site for which you're responsible. However, no matter where you work or what type of site you're working on, you need to know Hypertext Markup Language (HTML), the language used to write Web pages, and you need to know it inside out. That's the bad news. The good news is that HTML is relatively easy to learn. You don't have to be a programmer or a computer scientist to figure it out.

As well as writing Web pages in HTML, the Webmaster at an organization is often responsible for administering the Web server, which is basically just a souped-up computer with some special software installed on it. Administering a

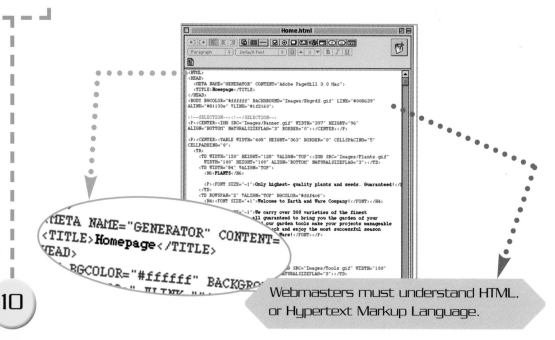

Webmasters must understand HTML, or Hypertext Markup Language.

10

server can be very simple or very complex, depending on the type of server it is and the way the network is set up. You'll learn more about networks and Web servers in the next chapter.

If the Web site uses a lot of multimedia, databases, or interactive features, the Webmaster may also need to be a full-fledged computer programmer. If you're interested in computer programming, the Web offers lots of opportunities. As a software development environment, the Web is very exciting and challenging because of the wide range of users and platforms supported. (If you're a closet technophobe, don't panic, because not all sites require these features.)

Quite apart from computer languages, it is always help-
ful for a Webmaster to be proficient in English. Part of a
Webmaster's job is something called content development,
which often involves
writing, editing, and
coordinating with non-
technical people.
Strong communication
skills are a real asset
in this field.

**Webmaster or
Webmistress?**

Whether you're
male or female, the
preferred usage is
Webmaster. After all,
skills are mastered,
not mistressed.

Finally, it never
hurts for a Webmaster
to have a flair for
graphic design. Even if
you're working with a designer, there are some tricks to
designing and producing graphics for the Web that the
Webmaster needs to know.

There are tons of other attributes that make a good
Webmaster, such as having a sense of humor, a taste for
adventure, a lot of creativity, and a willingness to experi-
ment. The Web is still very new. Nobody can say for sure
where it will lead, but it's up to you to blaze the trail.

chapter two

NETWORK BASICS

A Web site is really nothing more than a collection of electronic files on a computer. You can have a Web site on a personal computer that's not even connected to a network, but what fun would that be? The whole point of having a Web site is to share information, and the best way to share information between computers is through a network.

There are lots of different types of computer networks, and there are people called network engineers whose job it is to design and build them. You don't need to be a network engineer to be a Webmaster, but you do need to understand some network basics.

So, what is a computer network? It's exactly what it sounds like. A network can be two computers or two million computers. The computers can be connected by cables and wires, by modems, or

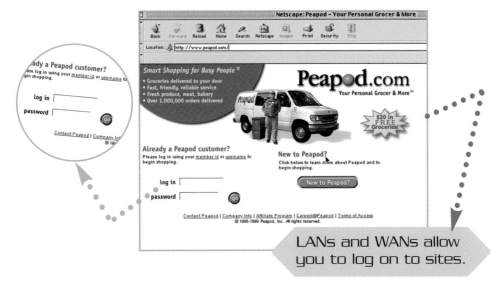

13

by infrared signals. Wherever and however computers "talk" directly to each other, a computer network exists.

Two very common types of networks are local area networks (LANs) and wide area networks (WANs). These are the private computer networks that organizations use to share information among their members. LANs and WANs differ mostly in how close the computers are to each other. For example, a network of computers that are all in the same building but on separate floors would be a LAN. A network of computers that are all in the same organization but in separate cities would be a WAN.

These are very generic terms that encompass a huge variety of networks, but don't worry about that. The only LANs and WANs you need to worry about are the ones that use the Transmission Control Protocol/Internet Protocol (TCP/IP).

What?!

Well, before computers can really communicate with each other, they need to have a common language or an agreed-upon set of rules. When a diplomat goes to a foreign country, he or she follows a special set of rules and customs called a protocol. Computers do a similar thing when networking with other computers. The set of customs computers follow when they interact with each other is also called a protocol.

Now, to really complicate matters, you can have a computer network that uses lots of different protocols at the same time. This isn't as confusing as it sounds, and it happens all the time in human social networks. For example, you are probably a member of a family that has certain rules and customs (protocols), which are not exactly the same as the rules and customs practiced by the family down the street. They, in turn, have customs that are different than the family next door. However, all three families co-exist in the same neighborhood, and all three families manage to abide by the rules and customs of the city and the country where they live. Human networks are complicated and rely on many layers of protocol to work. Computer networks are no different in that respect.

There are hundreds of different network protocols, but you don't need to know about them all. The networks you'll be most concerned with as a Webmaster are the ones that use the TCP/IP and the hypertext transfer protocol (HTTP). TCP/IP networks include intranets, extranets, and, as you probably already guessed, the Internet itself.

THE INTERNET ▶▶▶▶▶▶▶▶▶

The Internet is a public computer network, and it's the biggest network in the world. It's actually a collection of smaller networks that are all networked together (it used to be called the Inter-Networked Network, but that was just too many syllables, so it got shortened to Internet). It's hard to say how big the Internet is at any given time, because it depends on how many people are connected to it. If you use a modem to dial up and connect to the Internet from your home computer, your computer becomes part of the Internet for as long as you're connected. It works like this: Your modem connects your computer to another computer, which, in turn, is connected to the Internet.

INTRANETS ▶▶▶▶▶▶▶▶

An intranet uses TCP/IP, just like the Internet. Unlike the Internet, however, intranets are private. You can't connect to or use an intranet without permission. Unauthorized users are kept out by something called a firewall. A firewall is a computer program that works like an electronic fence. You need the right key to get in or out. Intranets aren't much different than LANs or WANs. In fact, they are really just LANs and WANs that use TCP/IP.

EXTRANETS ►►►►►►►►►►

If the Internet is public, and intranets are private, then extranets are somewhere in between. Organizations use extranets to share information with people who don't have or need access to an intranet yet need more privacy or security than the public Internet provides. This is called an extranet because it's external, or outside of the organization's traditional computer network. There is a firewall between the Internet and the extranet and another firewall between the extranet and the intranet. An extranet is sometimes called a demilitarized zone because it's a neutral territory between two firewalls.

Imagine that a company has a dozen traveling sales representatives scattered around the country. The salespeople all have laptop computers and modems, but because they are in different hotel rooms every night, it's not possible to give them LAN or intranet access. Before they had an extranet, the salespeople entered the orders on their laptops, printed them out, and faxed them to the warehouse. Someone at the warehouse then had to enter them into the shipping database. Now, the salespeople just connect to the Internet, which con- nects them to the extranet, where they enter their orders directly into the

The Internet is the place to be if you want to be seen.

shipping database. The shipping department then uses the company intranet to retrieve the orders from the extranet.

When most people think about building Web sites, they think about the Internet, and who can blame them? The Internet is high profile, and if you want to be seen, it's the place to be. However, intranets and extranets are growing at an amazing pace, and there is every indication that they are becoming indispensable tools to businesses of all types and sizes. If you want a good, stable job building Web sites, intranets and extranets provide good opportunities as well.

chapter three

SERVERS, BROWSERS, AND PROTOCOLS

You remember from the last chapter that TCP/IP is the network protocol used by the Internet, intranets, and extranets. You also remember that networks can use a lot of different protocols at the same time. It might help to think of these protocols as layers. TCP/IP is the basic layer that lets computers talk to each other. On top of the TCP/IP layer are other protocols that let computers do specific things, such as send and receive e-mail or serve Web pages.

WHAT IS A WEB SERVER? ▶▶

A Web server is a computer that "serves" Web pages, just like a waiter in a restaurant serves food.

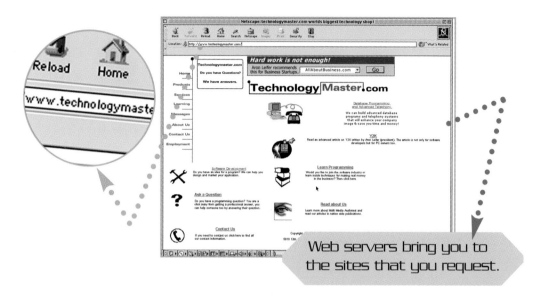

Web servers bring you to
the sites that you request.

It stays open twenty-four hours a day, waiting for orders to come in from the Internet. When someone "orders" a Web page, by clicking on a hypertext link, for instance, or by entering a URL into his or her browser, the Web server responds by sending the file. As soon as the file is sent, the Web server forgets about it and starts waiting for the next request.

That's all Web servers do. They serve files. It's a pretty boring job when you think about it.

A Web server may get only a few requests in a day or it may get millions. Some servers aren't much different from desktop PCs, but sites that get a lot of traffic need more powerful computers to operate efficiently. Some servers get so many requests that they need to be spread across many powerful machines. Whatever the size or power of a Web server, it uses the hypertext transport protocol, or HTTP, to send files and receive requests for files.

The only difference between a Web server and a regular PC is software. Web server software is what allows the computer to create connections to other computers to send them files. The type of Web server software you use depends on the type of computer you have.

Just as a program written for a Windows PC won't work on a Macintosh computer, Web servers designed for one hardware platform, or operating system, doesn't always work on another. Before you decide on your Web server software, you need to know what platform you'll be using. The most common platforms on the Web are Unix, Linux, and Windows NT.

COMMON WEB SERVER CONFIGURATIONS

Platform	Web Server
Linux	Apache/ Netscape Enterprise Server
Unix	Apache/ Netscape Enterprise Server
Microsoft Windows NT	Microsoft Internet Information Server

Learning to administer a Web server is like learning any other software program. It takes time and practice, but there is nothing magic about it. Like many other life skills, it's easy once you know how. People who don't

Administering a Web server is easy once you know how.

understand what you do may call you a magician or a computer genius. There is no need to tell them otherwise!

WEB BROWSERS ▶▶▶▶▶▶▶▶

The Web server software runs on the Web server, but people who are surfing the Web need software on their computers, too. A Web browser is an application that lets people view, or browse, the files that are on Web servers. The relationship between a Web browser and a Web server is sometimes called client/server, with the Web browser being the client and the Web server being the server. A Web server has clients, just like a doctor or a lawyer has

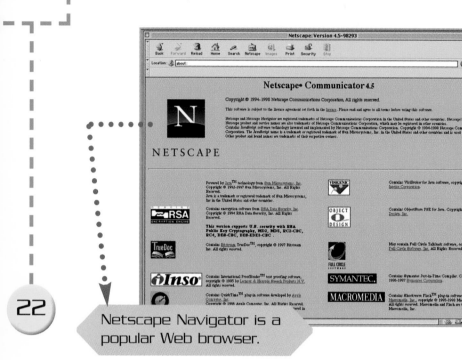

Netscape Navigator is a popular Web browser.

clients. The browser is called the client because it is using the services of the Web server.

There are a lot of different Web browsers out there, just as there are a lot of different Web servers. The two most common Web browsers are Netscape Navigator and Microsoft Internet Explorer. Both of these programs read, interpret, and display Web pages, but they each do these things a little bit differently. One of a Webmaster's biggest challenges is to understand how different Web browsers display things. We will talk more about that in chapter five, but first things first.

chapter four

CONTENT IS KING

A Web site needs a reason to exist, and for most sites the reason is to convey information. Information can take a variety of forms. It might be in text, images, sounds, data, or a combination of all of these. Part of a Webmaster's job is to collect information and organize it in such a way that people can find what they are looking for. This process is called content development.

However, before you even start developing content, your Web site needs to have a mission and some goals. Your goals will determine what content you need for your site, not the other way around. The first step is to sit down and talk to key people at your organization. Find out what their expectations are. What do they hope to accomplish by having a Web site? Are they hoping to increase sales? Improve communication among employees? You'll need to ask a lot questions and really listen to the answers.

Once you know what the goals are, you can start thinking about how the Web can help accomplish them. If the goal is to increase sales, then maybe an online storefront is the answer. Then again, maybe expanding customer service options on the Web will do more than a storefront to increase sales. The point is to be creative, think about the long term, and don't assume that your first instinct is right (maybe it is, and maybe it isn't).

Once you have your goals and you've decided how the Web can help, the next step is to think about the audience. Who are your customers, and how will they use your site? If you are trying to sell medical supplies to doctors, your site will be a lot different from, say, a site

Determine your Web site's goals and audience.

that is selling music CDs. Different audiences have different needs. Your job is to figure out what your audience needs.

One way to do this is to create some user scenarios. This is a lot of fun. Make up some fictional charac- ters to represent the typical users of your site. Give them names, personalities, biographies, hairstyles, astrological signs, or whatever you need to do to make them real. Then describe each of these people as they visit your Web site for the first time. What buttons do they push? Where do they go? What are they looking for? Do they search for specific things or are they just brows- ing? Do they start throwing stuff in their virtual shopping carts immediately?

With a handful of user scenarios developed, you should have some pretty good insight into how people will use your site. Use this knowledge to create a "laundry list," or content list. This is just an unorganized list of all the information your site will need to include. Do you need a sample sound file to "tease" customers into buying a CD? Write it down. Do you need a picture of the CD cover? Write it down. A quote from the artist? A picture of the band? A concert schedule? A link to the official fan club's home page? Write it all down.

Once you have a content list, it's time to start organizing your site. Divide your site into sections by arranging the items on your list in logical groupings. For example, all the items mentioned above are things that help the user decide what to purchase. You might have a separate logical grouping of items that help the user learn how to purchase. This would include your payment policies and procedures, preferred shipping methods, and so on. You might also have a customer service section, where people can check on the status of their orders after they have made a purchase.

Create a content list of your site's information.

Would it make sense to put all the pictures on one page and all the related text on another? Of course not. The key is to arrange your content items in a way that makes sense. This is a lot like making an outline for a research paper. Get out your pens and paper and draw arrows back and forth to indicate links between pages. When you're all done, you'll have something called a site map. This is your blueprint. You'll refer to it again and again as you build and refine your Web site.

It may seem like a bore, but the work you do at this stage to organize your site will pay off for your users down the road.

A detailed site map is essential as you build and refine your site.

chapter five

BUILDING YOUR SITE

In your surfing around the Web, you have no doubt noticed that a lot of Web addresses (technically called URLs) end in the ".html" extension. That's because all Web pages are written in something called HTML, which stands for Hypertext Markup Language.

ABOUT HTML ▶▶▶▶▶▶▶▶▶

HTML isn't really a programming language. It's called a markup language, because you use it to "mark up" text, just as if you were writing notes in the margins of a sheet of paper. When you format a page in HTML, all you are doing is writing a set of instructions about how the text is supposed to look. In HTML, these instructions are called tags.

An HTML tag is enclosed in brackets. There is usually an opening tag and a closing tag. For example, if you wanted the words *My Home Page* to appear in bold type, then the HTML code would look like this:

<b>My Home Page</b>

When a Web browser, such as Netscape Navigator, receives a Web page from a Web server, it reads through the HTML code and follows the instructions it finds there. Remember that every Web browser can interpret tags a little bit differently. For example, there is an HTML tag that opens with <strong> and closes with </strong>. One browser might display everything between these tags as italic, while another browser will display it as bold.

The differences in the way Web browsers interpret and display pages are known collectively as browser compatibility issues. If you are an intranet developer and you have some control over what Web browsers are being used within your organization, these issues may not affect you very much. However, if your Web site is on the Internet, where anybody with any Web browser can visit, you will need to have a very good understanding of browser compatibility issues.

You use HTML to deliver all types of content on the Web, not just text. You can include, or embed, sound files, image files, video clips, or all of those things. You can write HTML with any word processing program, and there are lots of good

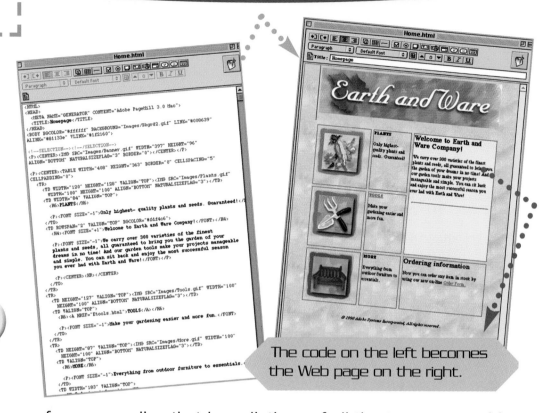

The code on the left becomes the Web page on the right.

references on-line that have listings of all the tags you would ever want to use. There are also a lot of software programs that will write the HTML for you. These programs are called HTML editors. You will want to become familiar with using some of them. They can save a lot of time, but like any short-cut, they can get you lost sometimes. HTML editors aren't magic, and you will still need to know your way around HTML.

Looking at other people's code is a great way to learn about HTML. To see what the HTML code looks like for any page in Netscape, go to the View menu and select Document Source. In Internet Explorer, go to the View menu and select Source.

GRAPHICS ON THE WEB ▶▶▶▶▶▶▷

Even if you work with a graphic designer to create your Web site, you may need to teach them a thing or two about graphics on the Web. Designers are good at designing, but they may not know what file formats to use or how to make images that load quickly in the user's browser.

Images can make all the difference between a dry, boring site and a site that is appealing to the eye. However, every one of those images translates into extra time that your users have to wait to see your Web site, and the bigger your images, the longer the wait. That's why you should do everything you can to make sure that the file sizes of your images are as small as possible. The tricks to this are choosing the right compression format and using "browser-safe" colors.

The two most common types of images on the Web are GIFs (in graphic interchange format) and JPEGs. The file name of GIF images always ends in ".gif," while the file name of JPEGs ends in either ".jpeg" or ".jpg." GIFs and JPEGs are images that have been compressed, or made smaller, with different compression formats. JPEG compression works really well for photographs. GIF compression works well for text and artwork that doesn't have a lot of color gradations. There are whole books devoted to what formats work for what and why, but don't worry about that yet.

You just need to know that if a designer gives you an image in another format (such as TIFF or EPS) you will need to convert it to GIF or JPEG before you can use it on the Web.

There are millions of colors in the world, but there are only 216 colors on the Web. That's because a lot of older computers can display only 256 colors, and the computer's operating system demands exclusive use of some of those. When the math is all done, there are 216 colors that look more or less the same on all computers, no matter what type of monitor, Web browser, or operating system the user has. These 216 colors are known as the browser safe colors. If you use a color that isn't one of these, the user's computer will "interpret" the color. Not only will this take longer, but the interpreted color may be nothing like your original intention.

By using the browser safe palette and the most appropriate compression format, your images will load faster, your users will have more fun, and you'll be assured that your site at least resembles your intended design.

Scanning is an easy way to add images to your Web site.

chapter six

INTERACTIVE AND DYNAMIC SITES

Dynamic. Interactive. Those words get thrown around a lot when people talk about the Web, but what do they really mean?

An interactive Web site is one that responds in some way to user input. If you click on a hypertext link, a Web site responds to your input by taking you to a different page. You can create an even higher level of interactivity by using Web-based forms. A Web form accepts user input, such as customer suggestions and feedback.

When most people talk about an interactive site, they are really talking about a dynamic site. A dynamic Web site is one that customizes its response based on user input.

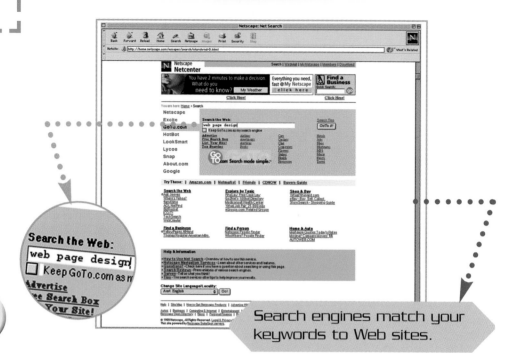

Search engines match your keywords to Web sites.

For instance, if you visit any search engine on the Web and type in some keywords, the search engine will respond by showing you a list of Web sites that match your keywords. It doesn't show you a list of all the sites on the Web or a list of sites matching anyone else's keywords. It is not just interactive but also dynamic. It creates a custom response based on your unique input.

To create its custom response, a dynamic Web site usually calls on some sort of database. It takes the user's request, checks its database for possible matches, and then creates a custom HTML page in response.

Creating a dynamic Web site requires some experience

with databases and knowledge of at least one scripting or programming language. Some scripting and programming languages commonly used to create dynamic sites include PERL, JavaScript, Java, Active Server Pages (ASP), Cold Fusion, and many others. Which application development environment you choose will depend on your Web server, your database, and your specific needs.

Programming for the Web is sometimes called

Register at Our Site

Name

Mailing Address

City

State

E-mail Adress

Country

Phone Number

Zip Code (U.S. only)   Your Age

Your Gender
● Male ○ Female

Send

Some sites require that visitors register to gain full access.

CGI programming, which is short for common gateway interface. Whenever you request a Web page from a Web server, you send that Web server a bunch of information about your computer system, such as what Web browser software you are using, where your computer is located on the Internet, and where you are coming from. This set of information, known as the CGI variables, can be used by programmers to customize a Web site just for you.

chapter seven

BEING SEEN

You can have the coolest site in the universe, but what good is it if nobody ever sees it? And how do you know who's looking at it?

The Webmaster at an organization is usually responsible for keeping track of how a Web site is used and how often it is used. If it is an Internet site, you may also be responsible for making sure that a site is available on search engines, so the people who want to know about your site can find it.

STATISTICS ▶▶▶▶▶▶▶▶▶▶

Your Web server software automatically generates something called a log file. Whenever someone on the Internet or intranet requests a file, the Web server puts this information in its log file. These file requests, sometimes known as hits, can add up very fast. A log file in itself is way too long and confusing to be very useful, but there are lots of different software programs that will analyze the log file and summarize statistics. These statistics are what the

Run weekly and monthly statistical reports for your site.

most requested files were, how long the average user spent on the site, how the users got to your site, and more.

It's a good idea to run weekly and monthly statistical reports for your site. By becoming familiar with usage patterns, you can learn to detect problems early on and correct them before they become disasters.

SEARCH ENGINES ▶▶▶▶▶▶▶▶

If your Web site is on the Internet, you will want to make sure that other people can find it. Adding your site to search engines is one of the best ways to ensure that the people who might be interested in your site can find it. Adding your site is easy. You just go to a search engine and follow the link to add, suggest, or submit a site. The problem is that it is very time consuming to visit every search engine and submit your site individually to each one.

There are several commercial services that will submit your site to hundreds of search engines for a small fee. If there is money in the budget for this, it will be money well spent.

However, before you register your site, you'll want to make sure that the search engines will index it correctly. Meta tags are a special kind of HTML tag that you can use to describe your site to search engines. The information you use in meta tags doesn't display on the Web page, but search engines can access it to find out how to categorize your site.

Meta tags allow you to specify the keywords that people can use to search for your Web page or to provide a brief synopsis (summary) of your Web site that can be displayed in the search results.

You can count the number of visitors to your site.

chapter eight

GETTING A JOB

Webmastering is a new career, and there aren't yet any hard and fast rules about what sort of training or education a Webmaster should have. The job requirements can vary as greatly as the job descriptions. Although it can't hurt to have a degree in computer science, it's certainly not a prerequisite. Where you got your skills matters less than the skills themselves.

So where do you get the skills? If you want to focus on the programming aspect of Webmastering, most colleges offer courses in computer sciences and computer programming. However, if your interest is mostly in server administration, you may also want a computer science department that offers an Internet track, with classes in Web server administration, HTML, CGI programming, and content development.

In the meantime, because there is no standard, formalized training available, aspiring Webmasters are left to learn their trade however and wherever they can. Community and technical colleges usually offer courses on Web server administration and basic program-

Most colleges offer courses in Web administration.

ming, including HTML. If you are a self-motivated learner, the Internet itself is your best classroom. Study other Web sites and look at their source code. Join on-line discussions about technology issues. Read news stories and tutorials and anything else that expands your knowledge.

Some software companies offer tests that certify you to use or administer their software. You pay the company to take the test, and if you pass, they issue you a certificate. Depending on the type of Web servers being used, some employers may want you to have certifications from Microsoft or Sun.

For the most part, companies that are looking to hire a Webmaster will be interested in your attitude, your enthusiasm, and samples of your work. Have finished Web sites ready. Volunteer to build a Web site for your school, neighborhood association, church, chess club, or your uncle Fred. Build a personal home page for yourself. Before you know it, you will have a portfolio of Web sites you can show to potential employers, and this, more than anything else, will tell them what sort of Webmaster you can be.

Being a Webmaster is a fun, demanding, and exhausting job. It's also very exciting, because you are helping to build a brand new industry. You might have to work overtime once in a while, especially when you are close to launching a site, but on the up side, you probably won't have to wear a suit to work. High-tech companies, especially, are dominated by creative workers and a relaxed, casual work environment.

Explore the Web now to help you get started on your future career.

The World Wide Web is the marketplace and the media of tomorrow, and it's waiting for you to make your mark.

WORDS.COM: GLOSSARY

client   Any computer connected to an Internet server. When you request a Web page from a Web server, your computer becomes a client of that Web server. A computer program is sometimes called a client, too, as in e-mail client.

cyberspace   Another word for the Internet.

domain   A particular named area of the Internet. This can be a Web domain, as in *www.domain.com*, or part of an e-mail address, as in janejoe@domain.com.

download   To transfer a file from the Internet to your computer.

dynamic   Changeable. A dynamic Web site is automatically generated based on user input, as opposed to a static site, which stays exactly the same until the Webmaster changes it.

e-commerce   Sales and business conducted over the Internet.

e-mail   Abbreviation for electronic mail.

extranet A computer network that is linked to both a private organization and outside networks.

firewall A computer program that keeps computer networks secure.

FTP (file transfer protocol) Just like it sounds, this protocol is designed to handle the transfer of any type of file over the Internet.

HTML (Hypertext Markup Language) The language used to create files to be viewed on the World Wide Web.

HTML editor An application that helps you to create HTML files.

HTTP (hypertext transport protocol) The protocol used by the World Wide Web.

hypertext link A text or graphic on a Web page that, when clicked, takes you to another page on the Web.

intranet A computer network that is used privately.

ISP (internet service provider) Any company or institution that provides access to the Internet.

keyword A word or phrase used for searching.

protocol In computer talk, as in diplomacy, this is an accepted standard for behavior and/or communication.

remote host A computer you are connected to that is not in the same physical location. Also known as a remote server.

search engine A program or Web site that searches the Internet for appropriate sites, based on keywords entered by the user.

server   A computer that is permanently connected to the Internet. When you connect to the Internet, you are connecting to a server that acts as your gateway to the Internet.

static   Fixed, unchanging. A static site is one that is written in straight HTML, as opposed to a dynamic site, which is automatically generated based on user input.

upload   To transfer a file from your computer onto the Internet.

Web address   The place on the Internet where a particular file can be found. Web addresses always start with "http://" followed by the domain name. For example, *http://www.mydomain.com.* Also known as URL (Uniform Resource Locater).

Web browser   An application for viewing Web pages.

Webmaster   Someone who builds or maintains a Web site.

Web server   A computer that serves, or delivers, Web pages.

Web site   A page or a collection of pages on the World Wide Web.

World Wide Web   The part of the Internet that can be displayed in graphic format.

RESOURCES.COM: WEB SITES

The Browser Safe Color Palette
http://www.lynda.com/hex.html

JavaScript Developer Central
http://developer.netscape.com/tech/javascript/index.html

Web Review: An E-zine for Webmasters
http://www.webreview.com/

World Wide Web Consortium
http://www.w3c.org/

The Yale C/AIM Web Style Guide
http://info.med.yale.edu/caim/manual/

The Beginner's Guide to HTML
http://www.ncsa.uiuc.edu/General/Internet/WWW/
      HTMLPrimer.html

BOOKS.COM: FOR FURTHER READING

Cook, Peter, and Scott Manning. *Why Doesn't My Floppy Disk Flop? And Other Kids' Computer Questions Answered by the Compududes.* New York: John Wiley & Sons, 1999.

Levine, John. *The Internet for Dummies.* Indianapolis, IN: IDG Books, 1998.

McCormack, Anita L. *The Internet: Surfin' the Issues.* Springfield, NJ: Enslow, 1998.

Morris, Mary. *Cybercareers.* Englewood Cliffs, NJ: Prentice Hall Computer Books, 1997.

Spainhour, Stephen, and Valerie Quercia. *Webmaster in a Nutshell: A Quick Desktop Reference.* Cambridge, MA: O'Reilly & Associates, 1997.

Weinman, Lynda. *Designing Web Graphics 2.* Indianapolis, IN: New Riders Publishing, 1997.

Williams, Robin. *The Non-Designer's Web Book: An Easy Guide to Creating, Designing, and Posting Your Own Web Site.* Berkeley, CA: Peachpit Press, 1997.

INDEX

CREDITS

ABOUT THE AUTHOR

Marty Brown is a Webmaster and database programmer. She has developed numerous sites for businesses and the government on both intranets and the Internet. She is currently the Webmaster of Timber Press, Inc. Brown has a B.A. in Liberal Arts from The Evergreen State College and a M.S. in Publishing Studies from New York University. She lives in Portland, Oregon, with her son, his father, and two cats.

PHOTO CREDITS

Cover photo © Superstock; p. 7 by Shalhevet Moshe; pp. 17, 21, 27, 41 by Karen Tom; p. 24 © International Stock; p. 26 by Steve Skjold; pp. 32, 40 by Thaddeus Harden; p. 37 © Superstock.

LAYOUT AND DESIGN

Annie O'Donnell